D0594123

THIS
BOOK
BELONGS
TO
DATE

The Books About Felicity

Meet Felicity · An American Girl

Penny, the horse Felicity loves, is in trouble. Felicity must figure out a way to help her before it's too late!

Felicity Learns a Lesson · A School Story

Lessons about serving tea pose a problem for Felicity—how to be loyal to her father and to her friend.

Felicity's Surprise · A Christmas Story

Felicity's mother becomes terribly ill. Is Christmastide really a time when hopes and dreams come true?

Happy Birthday, Felicity! · A Springtime Story

Felicity overhears a message that means danger to the colonists, and she must warn them herself.

Felicity Saves the Day · A Summer Story

Felicity's friend Ben has run away and needs help. Will Felicity help Ben—or tell her father where he is?

Changes for Felicity · A Winter Story

Felicity faces many changes in her friendships and her family as war breaks out in the colonies.

Meet Felicity

An American Girl

By Valerie Tripp

Illustrations Dan Andreasen

Vignettes Luann Roberts, Keith Skeen

Pleasant Company

Published by Pleasant Company Publications Incorporated

For information, address: Book Editor,
Pleasant Company Publications Incorporated,
8400 Fairway Place, P.O. Box 620998,
Middleton, WI 53562.

First Edition.
Printed in the United States of America.
94 95 96 97 98 RRD 12 11 10

PICTURE CREDITS
The following individuals and organizations have generously given permission to reprint illustrations contained in "Looking Back": pp. 64-65–*The Copley Family,* John Singleton Copley, National Gallery of Art, Washington, Andrew W. Mellon Fund; Virginia State Library and Archives; The New York Historical Society, N.Y.C.; Courtesy Massachusetts Historical Society; pp. 66-67–Colonial Williamsburg Foundation (garden, house, wig); *Sir Edward Walpole's Children,* Stephen Slaughter, The Minneapolis Institute of Arts; Colonial Williamsburg Foundation (lacing up stays, fan); pp. 68-69–Colonial Williamsburg Foundation (knife, epergne, plate); Courtesy of Charles Carter, Shirley Plantation, Charles City, Virginia; Courtesy Library of Congress; Abby Aldrich Rockefeller Folk Art Center; Colonial Williamsburg Foundation (worker, children on fence).

Edited by Jeanne Thieme
Designed by Myland McRevey and Michael John Victor
Art Directed by Kathleen A. Brown

Library of Congress Cataloging-in-Publication Data

Tripp, Valerie, 1951–
Meet Felicity: an American girl / by Valerie Tripp; illustrations, Dan Andreasen; vignettes, Luann Roberts, Keith Skeen.–1st ed.

p. cm.–(The American girls collection)
Summary: In Williamsburg in 1774, nine-year-old Felicity rescues a beautiful horse who is being beaten and starved by her cruel owner.

ISBN 1-56247-005-1—ISBN 1-56247-004-3 (pbk.)
[1. Horses–Fiction. 2. Williamsburg (Va.)–Fiction.]
I. Andreasen, Dan, ill. II. Title. III. Series.
PZ7.T7363Mc 1991 [Fic]–dc20 91-6449 CIP AC

TO MY MOTHER AND FATHER,
KATHLEEN AND GRANGER TRIPP

Table of Contents

Felicity's Family

Father
Felicity's father, who owns one of the general stores in Williamsburg.

Mother
Felicity's mother, who takes care of her family with love and pride.

Felicity
A spunky, spritely colonial girl, growing up just before the American Revolution in 1774.

Nan
Felicity's sweet and sensible sister, who is six years old.

William
Felicity's almost-three brother, who likes mischief and mud puddles.

Ben Davidson
A quiet apprentice living with the Merrimans while learning to work in Father's store.

Mrs. Fitchett
A friendly, gossipy customer at Mr. Merriman's store.

Penny
The spirited, independent horse Felicity loves.

Jiggy Nye
A cold-hearted scoundrel who mistreats his horse, Penny.

Marcus
The man who helps Mr. Merriman at home and at the store.

Chapter One

Merriman's Store

Felicity Merriman pushed open the door to her father's store and took a deep breath. She loved the smell of coffee beans and chocolate, of pine soap, spice tea, and apples. No other place in the world smelled as good as her father's store.

"Good day, Mistress Merriman!" said her father. He smiled and bowed.

Felicity grinned. Her father always pretended she was a fine lady customer when she came to his store. "Good day, Mr. Merriman," she answered. She liked to pretend, too.

"That's a lovely hat you are wearing, young miss. Have you come to buy a new feather for it?"

said Mr. Merriman. "Or perhaps you'd like some new ribbon or straw flowers?"

"Oh, Father! You know I don't fancy this old hat at all," giggled Felicity. "I wear it only because Mother insists." She pushed the straw hat off her head so that it hung down her back.

"Aye," agreed her father. "It's supposed to shade your face, so that the sun does not make your nose red."

Felicity rubbed her nose. It *was* rather pink. "I do forget to wear my hat sometimes," she said.

Mr. Merriman smiled. "Sometimes you forget and sometimes you are in too much of a hurry. I know my impatient girl. But don't fret. I think your nose is very pretty indeed." He tapped Felicity's nose with the tip of his finger. "And now, tell me. What did your mother send you to fetch today?"

Felicity stood very tall and pretended to be a fine lady again. "A penny's worth of ginger root, if you please, sir."

Her father bowed. "Yes, madam. Ginger it is," he said. "And here's a bit of rock candy for your trouble."

"Thank you, Father," said Felicity. She

popped the candy in her mouth and tasted its sharp sweetness. While her father weighed the ginger root and wrapped it in newspaper, Felicity looked around the store. The shelves were crowded with bolts of cloth, bowls, bottles, kettles, and coffee pots. Fat-bellied sacks of rice, flour, and salt leaned against barrels of nails.

Everywhere Felicity looked, she saw something useful or pleasing. There were aprons, night-caps, combs, spices, sponges, rakes, fishing hooks, tin whistles, and books. Felicity loved to daydream about the faraway places everything came from. The tulip bulbs came from Holland, the tea from China, and the cotton from India. Felicity believed her father's store was the finest store in Williamsburg and probably the finest store in all the thirteen colonies. The King of England himself didn't go to a better shop in London, Felicity was sure.

Mr. Merriman handed Felicity a neatly wrapped packet. "Here is your ginger, Lissie," he said. "Put it safe in your pocket so you won't lose it the way you lost the sugar last week."

Felicity put the ginger deep in her pocket. "I didn't quite *lose* the sugar, Father," she said. "I gave it away."

"To a horse!" laughed Mr. Merriman. "Ah yes, now I remember." He winked at his daughter. "I believe you'd give a horse anything. You do love horses, don't you, Lissie?"

"Aye!" said Felicity, nodding happily.

Mr. Merriman patted Felicity's pocket. "Mind you, don't give this ginger to any horse, or I'll be very disappointed. I'm hoping it's meant for a cake to go with my supper this evening. Hurry along home now, so you can help bake my ginger cake."

"Oh, must I go home, Father?" asked Felicity. Baking a ginger cake at home was not as interesting as helping in the store. Felicity loved to greet customers. Sometimes Father let her help them choose buttons and ribbons to buy. Sometimes she helped Marcus count the boxes and barrels of goods that had come in on ships from England. "May I stay here for a while?" Felicity asked. "May I help Marcus in the storeroom?"

"No, Lissie, you needn't stay," said Mr.

Merriman. "Have you forgotten? Ben helps Marcus in the storeroom now."

Hmph! thought Felicity. *Ben is so quiet and shy, 'tis easy to forget him.* Ben was the new apprentice. Father was teaching him how to run a store. Ben had come to live with the Merrimans one month ago. He slept in the loft above the stable and mostly kept to himself. Ever since Ben had come, Mr. Merriman did not need Felicity's help in the store at all.

Felicity sighed. She knew where she *should* be helping—at home. A pile of mending was waiting for her there. Felicity hated the idea of sitting straight and still, stitching tiny stitches, when all the while she was stiff with boredom. She would much rather stay at the store. But her father had already turned back to his work. There was nothing to do but go home.

Felicity was in luck. Just as she opened the door to go out, a stout, well-dressed lady sailed in. The lady's hat was decorated with ribbons and feathers that fluttered like leaves in a breeze. Felicity stepped back and held the door open wide.

"Mrs. Fitchett!" said Mr. Merriman happily. "What a pleasure! I haven't seen you since summer began. You look well!"

"Thank you, thank you, sir," said the lady cheerily. "You are looking well yourself." She nodded toward Felicity. "And who is this pretty maid?" she asked. "It's not your little Lissie, is it?"

Felicity smiled as her father answered, "Indeed, it is Felicity."

"Well, well!" Mrs. Fitchett gasped as if she were surprised. "The dear girl! Grown so tall and pretty! Hair as bright as a marigold! I am sure *she'll* have the lads flocking about, Mr. Merriman." Mrs. Fitchett turned to Felicity. "Are you ready for the lads to come a-courting, Miss Felicity? Are you working on your sampler of stitches to show them how well you sew?"

"No, ma'am," said Felicity. "I've not begun a sampler as yet."

"Not yet?" Mrs. Fitchett asked. "Why my two girls had finished their samplers when they were your age!"

"My Lissie's not much of a one for stitching," said Mr. Merriman. "She hasn't the patience."

"High-spirited, is she?" said Mrs. Fitchett. "Well, well, Mr. Merriman. Your girl will find her patience when she goes looking for it, I'm sure. Wait till she meets a fellow she fancies. She'll settle down fast enough."

"Lissie is far more interested in horses than fellows," smiled Mr. Merriman. "She'd rather go for a horseback ride than go to a fancy-dress ball." He looked at Felicity. "Isn't that true, Lissie, my girl?"

"Of course, Father!" said Felicity. She did not believe anyone could prefer dancing to riding horses.

"Horses!" exclaimed Mrs. Fitchett. "That reminds me why I came to your store today. I want to order oats for our horses to eat. Will you have your man bring a sack of oats 'round to my house, Mr. Merriman?"

"I'll have my new apprentice do it," said Mr. Merriman. "Ben is going to deliver a new bit and harness to Jiggy Nye at the tannery this afternoon. He will bring the oats to your house on his way."

"Very well," said Mrs. Fitchett. She lowered her voice to a gossipy tone. "I know why that good-for-nothing Jiggy Nye wants a new harness and bit. I hear he's got himself a new work horse. He won it gambling or

bit and bridle

some such thing. In any case, he didn't pay for it, mind you."

Felicity listened closely. She wanted to hear more about Mr. Nye's new horse. But Mrs. Fitchett frowned and said, "I believe he worked his old horse to death. That man is a cold-hearted scoundrel. He is not to be trusted. You'd better tell Ben to be sure Jiggy pays him for the harness right away."

"That I will," agreed Mr. Merriman. "I'll take no promises for payment from Jiggy. His money would be drunk up before I'd see it." Mr. Merriman glanced at Felicity and stopped talking. But Felicity knew all about Mr. Nye. Everyone knew he drank too much rum. When he did, he went into rages and left his work undone. His house was always a mess, and his fences were always falling down. Felicity didn't dislike him for any of those reasons. She hated Mr. Nye because he killed poor cows and horses that were too old to work anymore and made leather from their hides.

"What's Mr. Nye going to do with his new horse? He's not going to work it to death, too, is he, Father?" asked Felicity.

"Don't you worry about Jiggy Nye's new horse,"

*"I believe he worked his old horse to **death**," said Mrs. Fitchett. "He is not to be **trusted**."*

said Mr. Merriman. "I'm sure it's strong and healthy. Jiggy would be foolish to mistreat it." He kissed Felicity on the forehead. "Now you run along home. Your mother will be wondering what's become of you and that ginger. Good-bye, my child."

"Good-bye, Father. Good day, Mrs. Fitchett," said Felicity.

"Farewell, Miss Felicity," said Mrs. Fitchett.

Felicity stepped out into the bright afternoon. She walked home thinking only one thing. *Jiggy Nye has a new horse, and I'm going to see it—somehow—as soon as I can.*

CHAPTER
TWO

PENNY

Late afternoon sunshine slanted through the window onto Felicity's back. Felicity squirmed. She had a terrible itch and didn't know how to scratch it. She couldn't reach it with her left hand. Her right hand was inky, because she was practicing her script. She jiggled her shoulders up and down. She held her breath and rubbed her sides with her elbows. She leaned back and wiggled her shoulder against the chair.

"Felicity, my dear!" exclaimed her mother. "Why are you twitching and fidgeting so?"

"I have the most awful itch, Mother," said Felicity. "I think my stays are laced too tight today. They're so pinching and uncomfortable." Felicity pulled at her stays, which were laced up her back like a tight vest.

Mrs. Merriman shook her head and laughed. "You think your stays are laced too tight every day! But you do grow so fast, maybe you are right. Come here, my child, and I will loosen them for you."

"Thank you, Mother," said Felicity. She sighed with relief as her mother loosened the laces.

"I've told you many times, Lissie. Your stays will not pinch you if you sit up straight," said Mrs. Merriman. "And they will not be uncomfortable if you move gracefully instead of galloping about." She straightened Felicity's cap. "There, now, pretty one. You are set to rights. Fetch me your paper, so that I may see your handwriting practice."

Felicity blushed as she handed her mother the paper. "I haven't quite finished it, Mother," she said.

"So I see," said Mrs. Merriman. "The first few letters are very fine. But you lost patience when you got to the letter H. The rest of the letters go trip-trotting all over the page and then turn into sketches of horses!" She put the paper down and looked Felicity in the eye. "Lissie, what am I to do with you? You must learn to finish what you begin. If you spent half as much time on your letters as you do daydreaming of horses, you'd have the finest hand in Williamsburg." She sighed. "Go along to the well now. Fetch some water and scrub your hand. Mind you get the ink off."

"Yes, Mother," said Felicity. She turned to go, but stopped at the door. "Mother," she asked. "May I help Ben make a delivery?"

"Yes, my lively girl," laughed her mother. "I know very well there's no use trying to keep you inside when your mind is already out and away."

"Thank you, Mother!" said Felicity as she flew out the door.

"Lissie! Your hat!" called her mother. But she was too late. Felicity was already halfway to the well.

❧

Felicity's hand was still a little wet and a little inky when she rushed down the street to her father's store. Just as she got there, she saw Ben come out. He stopped and looked up the street toward the silversmith's shop, then down the street toward the church, as if he were not sure which way to go.

"Ben, do you know the way to Mrs. Fitchett's

house?" Felicity asked.

Ben shrugged. "I'll find it."

Ben's shyness didn't stop Felicity. "Come on," she said. "I'll show you."

Ben shrugged again. "As you wish," he said. Then he was quiet.

Felicity didn't mind. It was so lovely to be outside. And this was just the kind of afternoon she loved best. She could see a few leaves that had turned bright gold. They were like small banners announcing that summer's heat was ending and fall's cool weather was on its way.

Felicity was supposed to be leading Ben, but Ben took such long strides Felicity had to trot to keep up with him. Finally she lifted the hems of her petticoats so that she could take long strides, too. It felt wonderful to be able to stretch her legs.

"Oh, I wish I could wear breeches," she said.

"What?" asked Ben.

"Breeches," said Felicity. "Gowns and petticoats are so bothersome. I'm forever stepping on my hem and tripping unless I take little baby steps. Small steps are supposed to look ladylike. But I can't get

breeches

anywhere. 'Tis a terrible bother. In breeches your legs are free. You can straddle horses, jump over fences, run as fast as you wish. You can do anything."

Ben didn't answer, but he shifted the sack of oats to his other shoulder. Now Felicity could see his face.

"It's very tiresome to be a girl sometimes," Felicity went on. "There are so many things a young lady must not do. I'm told the same things over and over again. Don't talk too loud. Don't walk too fast. Don't fidget. Don't dirty your hands. Don't be impatient." Felicity sighed. "It's very hard. You're lucky to be a lad. You can do whatever you like."

Ben shook his head. "I *can't* do whatever I like. I'm an apprentice."

"Oh," said Felicity. They walked in silence for a while. Then Felicity asked, "Are you happy here in Williamsburg?"

"Happy enough," said Ben.

"I imagine you miss your family and friends back in Yorktown," said Felicity. "And I'm sure they miss you, too. If I loved someone, I could never let him go away from me. I would be too miserable and lonely." She glanced over at Ben. Maybe he was lonely. "You'll be happier here when you have some friends," she said.

"Aye," said Ben. Then he hid his face behind the sack of oats again.

Felicity and Ben made their way along the dusty, wide, main street of Williamsburg. It was not very busy this afternoon. The city was just beginning to wake up after the hot, sleepy summer. Mrs. Vobe was welcoming some guests to her tavern. The milliner had opened the windows of her shop to catch the first fall breezes. Here and there, peeking out from behind a hedge or a fence, Felicity saw yellow flowers nodding their heads to welcome autumn.

After they delivered the oats to Mrs. Fitchett's stable, Ben said, "I can find my way to the tannery and home from here."

Felicity kept right on walking. "Mr. Nye has a new horse, and I've a curiosity to see it," she said. Felicity half expected Ben to tell her to run along home, but he didn't say anything. *Sometimes I'm glad he's so quiet,* thought Felicity. She grinned to herself.

Jiggy Nye's tannery was on the far edge of the town, out where the neat fenced yards grew ragged and pastures stretched off into the woods. Felicity could smell the tannery vats before she could see the tumble-down tannery shed. The vats were huge kettles full of yellow-brown ooze made of foul-smelling fish oil or sour beer. Jiggy soaked animal hides in them to make leather.

"Whoosh!" said Felicity. "The smell of the tannery is enough to make your hair curl!"

"Aye!" said Ben. "The whole business stinks."

Suddenly they heard angry shouts and a horse's frightened whinnies.

"Down, ye hateful beast! Down, ye savage!" they heard Jiggy yell.

Felicity ran to the pasture gate. She saw Jiggy in the pasture, trying to back a horse between the shafts of a work cart. The horse was rearing up and whinnying. It jerked its head and pawed the air with its hooves. Jiggy was shouting and pulling on a rope that was tied around the horse's neck.

"I'll beat ye down, I will," yelled Jiggy. "I'll beat ye!"

Ben caught up with Felicity and pulled her arm. "Stay back," he ordered.

"No! I want to see the horse," said Felicity. She stood behind the open gate and stared. The horse was wild-eyed and skinny. Its coat was rough and matted with dirt. Its mane and tail were knotted with burrs. But Felicity could see that it was a fine animal with long, strong legs and a proud, arched neck. "Oh, 'tis a beautiful horse," whispered Felicity. "Beautiful."

Jiggy and the horse both seemed to hear her at the same moment. The horse calmed and turned toward Felicity. That gave Jiggy a chance to tighten the rope around its neck. When the horse felt the rope, it went wild again. Jiggy was nearly pulled off the ground when it reared up on its hind legs.

"Ye beast!" Mr. Nye shouted. He glared at Ben and barked, "Help me! Get in here and grab this rope!"

Ben darted into the pen and grabbed the rope with Jiggy, but the horse reared and pawed the air more wildly than before.

"I'll beat the fire out of ye!" shouted Jiggy in a rage. He raised his whip to strike the horse.

"No!" cried Felicity. At that, the horse took off across the pasture, dragging Ben and Jiggy through

"Stay back," Ben ordered.
"No! I want to see the horse," said Felicity.

the dust. They had to let go of the rope and give up.

Mr. Nye waved his arms and yelled at Felicity, "Get away with ye! You've spooked my horse, ye bothersome chit of a girl."

Felicity called out, "You spooked the horse yourself. You know you did!"

"Arrgh!" Mr. Nye snarled. He turned his red-rimmed eyes on Ben and growled, "What are ye doing here?"

"I've brought the bit you ordered from Master Merriman," Ben said.

Jiggy held out his hand. "Give it here."

Ben stepped back. "I'm to wait for payment," he said.

"Get away with ye!" shouted Mr. Nye. "Keep your blasted bit. That horse won't take the bit no matter. Go now, before I take my whip to the two of ye. Hear me?"

Ben turned to go, but Felicity backed away slowly. She couldn't stop watching the beautiful horse. It was running back and forth across the pasture, trapped inside the fence.

"Felicity, come along!" said Ben.

Felicity turned and followed Ben, but she did not

even see the road in front of her. "Isn't she beautiful, Ben?" Felicity said. "Isn't she a dream of a horse?"

"Aye," agreed Ben. "She's a chestnut mare, a blood horse."

"That means she's a thoroughbred, doesn't it?" said Felicity.

"Aye. It means she was trained to be a gentleman's mount," said Ben. "That horse is not bred to drag a work cart."

"She was never meant to belong to the likes of Mr. Nye!" Felicity exclaimed. "She's much too fine! Oh, just once I'd love to ride a horse like that!"

"She'd be too fast for you," said Ben. "You'd never stay on her." He shook his head grimly. "Besides, that horse won't trust anyone after the way Mr. Nye is treating her. She won't let anyone on her back ever again. That horse has gone vicious."

Felicity heard what Ben said, but she didn't believe it. She'd seen the look of frantic anger in the horse's eyes. But Felicity had seen something else, too. Under the wildness there was spirit, not viciousness. Just as under the mud and burrs there was a beautiful reddish-gold coat, as bright as a new copper penny. "Penny," whispered Felicity.

"What?" asked Ben.

"Penny," said Felicity. "That's what I'm going to call that horse. She's the color of a new copper penny. It's a good name for her, isn't it?"

"Aye," said Ben. "Because she's an independent-minded horse, that's for certain. Call her Penny for her inde*pen*dence, too."

Felicity smiled. From then on, she thought of the horse as Penny—beautiful, independent, bright, shining Penny.

By the time Felicity and Ben walked to the middle of town, the sun was melting on the horizon. They hurried along to the Merrimans' house.

"Felicity Merriman!" exclaimed her mother. "Wherever have you been all this time?"

"Ben and I stopped out at the tannery," said Felicity. "And, oh, Mother! We saw the most beautiful horse!"

"A horse?" asked Mrs. Merriman.

"It's Jiggy Nye's new horse, I wager," said Mr. Merriman.

Ben handed him the harness and bit. "Mr.

Nye didn't buy these things, sir. He can't control the horse enough to harness it. 'Tis a headstrong, independent-minded horse, a bright chestnut mare, and fast as fire."

"How did Jiggy Nye come to have such a horse?" asked Mrs. Merriman.

"No one knows for sure," said Ben. "Jiggy Nye says he won the horse in a bet from a man who found it straying in the woods. He says the man put a notice in the newspaper. The notice said that whoever lost the horse should come to claim it, but no one ever came. That's just Jiggy Nye's story, though. It's hard to trust his word."

Felicity had never heard Ben talk so much. She was surprised at all he knew.

"It's a pity Jiggy's got hold of the horse," said Mr. Merriman. He shook his head. "It will not end well, I fear."

Felicity could tell by the look on her father's face that Penny was in danger. She made up her mind to go back to the tannery and see Penny as soon as she could.

CHAPTER THREE

JIGGY NYE'S THREAT

September begins the season of thunderstorms in Virginia. For the next three days the sky was as gray as pewter, rain fell in sheets, and the wind roared around the corners of the house. Felicity felt as trapped as Penny was in Mr. Nye's pasture. "May I go out of doors, Mother?" she asked.

"In this storm?" her mother said. "Don't be a goose! The streets are all mud, and you'll be soaked to the skin in this rain. You will just have to wait till it stops."

Felicity sighed.

"Lissie, my love," said her mother. Her gentle voice sounded tired. "Look at this apron you sewed.

I've had to rip out the hem on it again. It's supposed to be twenty stitches to the inch, Lissie. And in a line. Yours fly all over. Your sister Nan sews more carefully, and she is but six years old."

"I'm sorry, Mother. Indeed I am," said Felicity. "My hands just won't go so slow."

Mrs. Merriman patted Felicity's hands and handed her the apron. "You will have to teach your hands to slow down, my girl," she said.

Felicity held up the apron and shook her head sadly. "All these miles and miles of stitches! They are never finished," she said.

"Slow and steady, my child," said her mother. "They'll be done faster if you do them right, so that you don't have to sew every seam twice. Remember, haste makes waste."

"Haste makes waste," Felicity repeated. She and her mother had to smile at each other, for Felicity was told that haste makes waste at least once every day of her life. She settled down to her stitching and tried very hard to be careful—for a little while.

At last the sun broke through the clouds, and Felicity was allowed to go outside.

"Take these preserves to Mrs. Deare," said her mother. "Nan and William will go with you. They've been cooped up, too."

Felicity hid her disappointment. She wanted to go see Penny by herself. She didn't want Nan and William dragging along. They were so slow! And she was so eager to see Penny. But she had no choice.

William toddled along on his fat little legs, dragging a stick through the mud. He stopped to pick up stones and drop them in puddles. He seemed to be trying to get as much mud on his shoes as he could. Nan walked in little ladylike steps, picking her way carefully around the puddles. Felicity was forever having to turn around and wait for careful Nan and muddy William.

"Oooh, Lissie," said Nan. "Look at the fine hat in the milliner's window! It has a whole bouquet of flowers on it! Let's go in and look at it."

"No! Come along, Nan," said Felicity. "I don't want to waste time with that foolishness."

Nan was miffed for a while, but she cheered up and put on her sweetest face when they reached Mrs. Deare's house. Mrs. Deare gave Nan and William each a cake. She fussed over them until Felicity thought she'd burst with impatience. Then, when they were at last on their way to the tannery, Nan announced, "I want to go home. I won't go any farther."

"Nan!" Felicity said sternly. "We're going to the tannery. Come along."

"No!" said Nan. "The tannery smells terrible. I won't go." She stuck out her lip.

"I won't, too," said William.

Felicity had an idea. "Nan," she said slowly. "There are lots of flowers out by the tannery. You can pick them and put them in your hat, so it will look just like the one in the milliner's window. Won't that be fine?"

"Well, perhaps," said Nan. "But I won't speak to that dirty old Mr. Nye. He's bad."

"Bad," repeated William. He swung his sticks as if they were swords.

Felicity led them along past Jiggy Nye's house to the pasture. And there was Penny! She was thinner, and her coat was even more matted and dirty. There was a red cut on one leg, as if she had hurt it trying to jump over the fence. Jiggy had tied Penny to a stake. The poor horse was straining at the rope, pawing the ground, and jerking and tossing her head.

"Horse!" said William.

"Yes," said Felicity. "Her name is Penny, because she's the color of a penny and because she's so inde*pen*dent."

"What does 'independent' mean?" asked Nan.

"It means she has a free spirit," said Felicity. "Penny wants to run." Felicity climbed up on the pasture fence.

"Don't go near her!" warned Nan.

"She won't hurt me. She will never hurt me," said Felicity. She called to Penny softly, slowly, "Penny! Penny, love. Look here. Look what I've brought you." Felicity tossed a lump of sugar close to Penny's nose.

"So much sugar, Lissie!" said Nan. "Where did you get it?"

"Hush!" said Felicity. She didn't take her eyes off Penny. "And don't tell about it when we get home, or—"

"So!" Mr. Nye's voice croaked in her ear. Felicity's heart stopped. Jiggy grabbed her by the shoulders and pulled her down off the fence. Nan knelt next to William and held him tight.

"You're that sly red-headed chit, ain't ye?" said Jiggy. "Didn't I tell ye to stay away from my horse?"

Felicity yanked herself out of his grasp. "I'm not hurting her," she said.

"This horse is none of your business, hear me?" growled Jiggy. "She's a vicious animal. She knocked the fence down trying to jump out of the pasture. I had to tie her up. I don't want ye spookin' her. Stay away!"

"You're that sly red-headed chit, ain't ye?" said Mr. Nye. "Didn't I tell ye to stay away from my horse?"

Felicity was frightened, but she was angry. "You are the one who scares the poor horse," she said to Jiggy. "You have no right to treat her so badly."

Jiggy grabbed Felicity again, but just then Penny whinnied wildly.

"Quiet, ye nag!" Jiggy shouted at Penny. He picked up a big stick and climbed into the pasture. As he came near, Penny reared. With a mighty pull, she broke the rope that tied her. Jiggy lost his balance and fell back into the dirt. He shook his fist at Penny as she ran away to the far end of the pasture.

"Ye worthless nag!" Jiggy yelled after Penny. His face was spattered with mud. "I'd give ye to anyone who can ride ye! *Anyone* can have ye! Hear me?" Jiggy stomped toward his house. Suddenly he turned toward Felicity and snarled, "And you! Get yourself and those brats out of here! I'll skin ye alive if I see ye here again." Then he stormed off.

Nan was crying. "Let's go! Please, let's go," she begged. She pulled on Felicity's petticoats and dragged her away. Felicity looked back to see Penny galloping around the pasture. At least Penny was not tied to the stake anymore. She was fenced in, but she could run and move. *Good for you, Penny,* thought Felicity. *Don't you let Mr. Nye scare you. I won't let him scare me!*

❦

At suppertime, it was William who gave it away. "Big horse," he said. "Bad man." He waved his spoon wildly.

"Shh," hissed Nan.

"What's all this?" asked Mother. "You've not been out to see that horse of Jiggy Nye's, have you?"

"Felicity made us go," said Nan. "And the horse made Mr. Nye fall down in the mud. Then Mr. Nye called the horse a nag, and he said anyone could take it if they could ride it. And he said he would skin us alive if we ever came back!"

"Hush, my child!" scolded Mrs. Merriman. "It's not proper to repeat such talk." She looked at Felicity, and her face was serious. "Jiggy Nye told you not to come back, and you won't—ever. His tannery is not a place for children."

"He was going to strike the horse with a big stick!" added Nan.

"The man's a villain of the worst sort," muttered Mr. Merriman. "A horse beater."

Ben spoke up. "He'll kill the horse, sir," he said. "Mark me, he will."

"Oh, Father," cried Felicity. "We can't let Mr. Nye hurt Penny! We've got to help her. We've got to get her away from Mr. Nye! Can't we buy her?"

"Gracious, no!" exclaimed her mother. "We've Old Bess for your father to ride, and Blossom to draw the cart."

"Bess is so slow, it's faster if you walk yourself!" said Felicity.

"Young lady," said Mrs. Merriman. "It would not harm you to go more slowly in all things—stitches and speeches and thinking, too."

Mr. Merriman spoke gently. "We've no need for a troublesome horse like that, my child. It would be useless to us, too. No one wants a horse that cannot be ridden. Besides, Marcus has enough to do with Old Bess and Blossom. He does not have time to care for another horse."

"But I would take care of her," said Felicity eagerly. "I would tame her and teach her. I would do everything."

Ben looked up.

Mrs. Merriman sighed. "Lissie," she said. "My impatient, headstrong Lissie. You have not the patience to sew a seam properly. You leave your writing practice half done. You lead your sister and brother to dangerous places and never stop to think. A willful girl and a willful horse is more than one family can handle. You must put that horse out of your head. Do you hear me?"

"Yes, ma'am," Felicity answered. For it was true, she did hear what her mother said. But she did not put the horse out of her head or her heart.

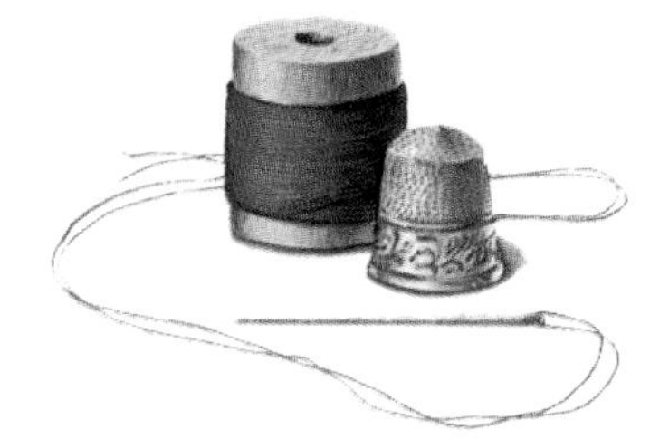

CHAPTER FOUR

BEN'S PROMISE

The last sliver of moonlight made a silvery path across the floor of Felicity's room. As soundlessly as in a dream, Felicity edged out of bed. She slipped her petticoats over her shift, pulled on her stockings and garters, and tip-toed to the door. Down the stairs she crept, skipping the step that creaked. She was shaking with nervousness.

It was better when she was outside. Felicity put on her shoes. Then she gathered her petticoats in her hand and ran fast through the garden, through the dark streets, past the sleeping houses. On she ran to the edge of town, where the trees grew close to the road and she was just another ghostly shadow.

By the time Felicity reached the pasture, she was

out of breath. She stood on the lowest rung of the fence and searched the darkness for Penny. The horse was tied to a stake by a thick rope. Penny looked up and tossed her head.

Felicity did not dare speak aloud. "I'm here. It's me," she whispered to Penny. "You don't have to trust me yet. But you will. I know you will."

Penny did not move. Felicity left a small apple near the stake. "Good-bye," she whispered. Then she ran home. The sky was only just beginning to grow light around the edges.

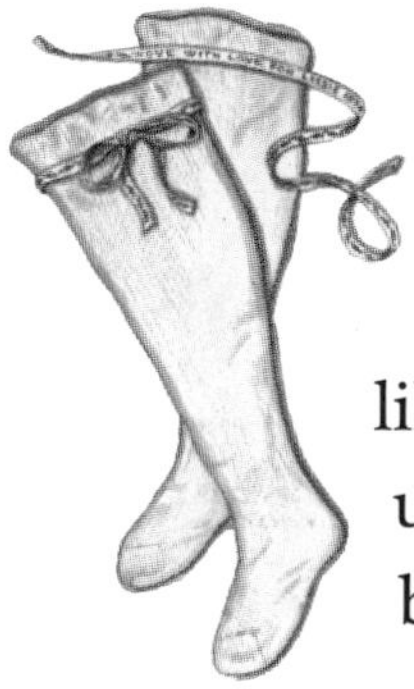

When Felicity came to breakfast, her mother looked at her. "Felicity!" she said. "Your petticoats are wet and muddy. Most likely your stockings are wet, too, all the way up to your garters. What on earth have you been doing?"

garters

Felicity looked down at her muddy hem. "I was just . . . just in the garden."

Mrs. Merriman smiled. "Digging around the pumpkins you planted?" she asked. "My impatient one! They'll not grow faster just to please you. Now sit down and eat your breakfast."

I need breeches, thought Felicity. *Then I can run*

freely. Then it won't matter if I get wet and muddy. But how can I get them?

She found the answer in the mending pile. It was a pair of Ben's breeches made of thin black cotton. Felicity knew Ben didn't wear these breeches very often, just to church sometimes. He wouldn't miss them if she borrowed them for a while.

The next morning before dawn, Felicity sneaked out of the house again. This time, she stopped by the stable. She had hidden Ben's breeches there, under an old bucket. She put the breeches on over her shift and tied them around her waist with a rope. Ben was skinny but tall, so the breeches went down to Felicity's ankles. As she ran through the silent streets toward the tannery, her legs felt so free! For once she could run as fast as she wanted to, without petticoats to hold her back.

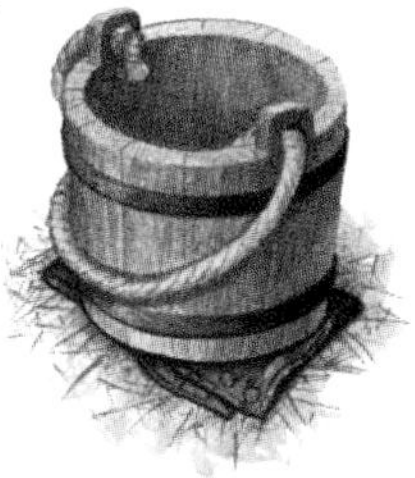

Morning after morning, before anyone was awake, Felicity slipped out of the house to visit Penny. At first, Felicity stayed outside the pasture. After a few days, she sat on the top rail of the fence. She sat near, but not *too* near, the stake to which Penny was tied. Felicity never spoke aloud. She

knew that if she were rough or noisy, she would frighten the horse. Even though Felicity couldn't sit still for her stitchery, she could sit almost without moving at all when she was near Penny. She felt peaceful, sitting on the rail fence those misty gray mornings, watching the beautiful horse. Sometimes Penny was calm. Sometimes she pulled on her rope or raised her head to sniff the wind. *She's thinking about running away,* thought Felicity. *She's thinking about freedom.*

The first time Felicity climbed off the fence into the pasture, Penny tossed her head and danced about. But she did not whinny or shy away. Soon Felicity thought Penny expected her to come each morning and maybe even looked forward to seeing her. Penny knew Felicity was kind and patient and would not hurt her. With all her heart, Felicity wished she had more time to spend with Penny so that the horse would trust her completely.

One morning after breakfast, Felicity was trying to hide her yawns as she practiced her stitches. She sat up straight when she heard her mother ask, "Ben, did you put your breeches in the mending pile, as I told you to?"

"Yes, ma'am," answered Ben.

"I don't see them there," said Mrs. Merriman. "Where are they?"

"I do not know, ma'am," said Ben.

"Well, look about you, lad!" said Mrs. Merriman. "Breeches don't just disappear!"

"Yes, ma'am," said Ben.

Felicity kept her head down but watched Ben out of the corner of her eye. He looked confused and a little embarrassed. *He has no idea what has happened to his breeches,* thought Felicity. *I wonder how he would feel if he did know?*

But no one knew Felicity's secret. No one knew about the lovely times she had with Penny all those dreamlike mornings. Felicity's secret made her happy. All day long, while she was mending or practicing her writing or playing with Nan and William, Felicity thought about Penny. The beautiful horse was growing more friendly every day.

Felicity always took an apple to Penny. One morning, after Felicity had been visiting her for a few weeks, Penny took the apple right from her hand. Felicity held her breath when she felt Penny's

warm nose tickling her fingers. She stood still. She did not try to touch Penny. From that time on, Penny made a game of asking for the apple. She would nudge Felicity gently and nicker until Felicity held the apple out to her.

On one drizzly morning, Penny nuzzled Felicity for the apple as usual. But before she took it, Penny raised her head, whinnied, and seemed worried. Felicity stepped back.

"What's wrong, Penny?" she whispered. Just then Felicity heard dogs barking and yowling. Jiggy Nye! He was coming out to the pasture!

Felicity dropped to the ground, rolled under the fence, and hid in the tall, scraggly grass. Penny whinnied and pawed the ground.

"Don't start with me, ye useless horse!" Jiggy snarled. He came into the pasture and stood by the fence, near Felicity's hiding spot. Felicity dared not move. Her heart thumped as she watched Jiggy put a bucket of water on the ground in front of Penny. "No oats till ye let me ride ye," he muttered to the horse. "Starve to death for all I care." As soon as Jiggy turned his back, Felicity got up and ran home as fast as she could.

But nothing—not even Jiggy Nye—could keep Felicity away from Penny. The mornings grew more chill as September blew into October. Felicity shivered when she pulled herself out of bed these mornings. But the sky stayed dark longer, so she had more time with Penny.

There was frost on the grass the morning Felicity untied Penny's rope from the stake and led her around the pasture for the first time. Penny followed behind Felicity, leaving the whole length of the rope between them. But after a week or so, Penny followed with her nose right next to Felicity's shoulder. Sometimes Penny even pushed at her playfully. At the end of their walks, Penny let Felicity stroke her neck and rub her nose.

"Aye, that's my girl," Felicity whispered in her ear. "You know I love you, don't you, Penny? Don't you, girl? You know I won't rush you."

The day came when all Felicity's patience was rewarded. One morning Penny was standing quietly next to the fence as if she were waiting for Felicity. Slowly, Felicity untied the rope from the stake.

Slowly, she climbed onto Penny's back. At first, Penny trotted. Felicity sat up straight and held on to her mane. As Penny's stiff trot eased into a smooth canter, Felicity leaned closer and closer to Penny's neck. Soon they were flying across the pasture, moving as swift and sure as the wind. Penny's hooves hardly seemed to touch the ground. Above them, the sky was pearly gray. The wind made Felicity's eyes water. She had moved that fast only in her dreams.

Every day Penny did something new. The first time Penny jumped over a small pile of hay, Felicity was so surprised she fell off the horse's back. After that, they tried higher and higher jumps—a heap of rocks, a tree stump, a stack of logs. Felicity never fell off again. She learned that Penny tensed her neck just before she jumped. That was a signal to Felicity to hold on tight.

Penny was full of surprises. One morning, she carried Felicity across the pasture in a gallop, then leaped effortlessly over the broken-down part of the fence. That morning they rode farther than ever before. Felicity lost track of time as they cantered deeper and deeper into the woods with no fences to stop them. When they jumped back over the fence, back into the pasture, Felicity re-tied Penny's rope to the stake quickly. She knew it was late. The sky was turning pink, and the mist was lifting out of the meadows.

Felicity ran home. She slipped into the stable as usual and changed from the breeches to her petticoats quickly. She was just rolling up the breeches to hide them under the bucket when she heard someone say, "You!"

It was Ben.

Felicity froze with the breeches in her hands. She

said nothing.

"What do you have there?" asked Ben in his coldest voice. He came forward. "What? *You* have my best Sunday breeches?" He took them out of Felicity's hands and looked at them. "They're wet and covered with mud!"

He sniffed them. "Whoosh! They smell like a horse!" He looked at Felicity. "Felicity, are you—"

Felicity interrupted him. "I'm sorry Ben. I was borrowing them. I just . . . I just needed them."

Ben sat down. "Felicity, tell me what you are doing," he said quietly.

Felicity took a deep breath. "I'm visiting Penny—the horse at the tannery."

"That horse?" said Ben. His eyes were wide.

"Oh, she's so fine, Ben," said Felicity. "She's gentle and dear. And she's so fast!"

"What!" Ben exclaimed. "You mean you're riding her?"

"Oh, yes!" said Felicity. "It's a wonder, Ben. It's just like riding the wind."

Ben shook his head. "Felicity, I don't know whether you are the bravest or the most foolish girl I've ever known," he said. "I'd be afraid to ride that horse. She looks like she would throw any rider sky-high!"

"She was afraid at first, but now she trusts me," said Felicity.

"How long have you been going out there?" Ben asked.

"Every day since the rain stopped," Felicity answered.

"That's almost one month!" Ben said. "You've been up before dawn, dressing in my breeches, and running out to see that horse for one month?"

"Yes."

Ben sat still. He stared at Felicity and said nothing. Then he asked, "How long can you keep doing this? You can't do it forever. Mr. Nye will surely see you someday. And Penny *is* his horse."

"I heard Mr. Nye say that anyone who could ride her could have her," said Felicity. "I can ride her. So she will be mine."

Ben sighed. "Felicity, you set your heart on things too much. I don't believe Mr. Nye or your father will let you keep that horse." He saw Felicity's stubborn frown, and he grinned. "But then I never would have believed you could have ridden that horse, either."

"I am going to get Penny away from Mr. Nye somehow," Felicity said. "I have to."

"Aye," said Ben. "You'd best do it soon."

"I can't hurry Penny," said Felicity. "I have to be patient with her."

Ben nodded.

"So, then," asked Felicity, "do you want your breeches back?"

"Not smelling the way they do!" laughed Ben. "No, you need them more than I do. You keep them as long as you like. I'll keep your secret."

"Thank you, Ben," said Felicity. She gave him a quick grin and hurried in to breakfast.

❧

Sharing Felicity's secret seemed to change Ben. He wasn't so shy. Sometimes he whistled, and he even surprised everyone by joking once or twice at supper. And he was true to his word.

That Sunday, Mrs. Merriman said, "Ben, have you still not found your good breeches? They were fine, expensive India cotton. 'Tis not like you to be so careless."

"I beg your pardon, ma'am," said Ben. "I know where they are now."

Felicity felt her face growing red. Was Ben going to tell?

"I lent them to a friend," said Ben easily.

"Indeed!" said Mrs. Merriman. "May I ask why?"

"My friend needs them more than I do," said Ben.

"Well," sighed Mrs. Merriman. "Dust off your old woolen breeches then. We needn't go to church looking like a band of ruffians."

Felicity smiled at Ben. He had called her his friend. He truly *was* a friend to her.

All that week, Felicity thought long and hard about what Ben had said. She knew he was right. She couldn't keep her secret much longer.

CHAPTER
FIVE

INDEPENDENCE

Felicity brushed Penny until she was as shining as the sun. She combed the horse's mane and untangled the knots in her tail. Jiggy Nye never brushed Penny, and usually Felicity was afraid to do more than pull the burrs off her coat. She did not want Jiggy to know someone was caring for Penny. But today was different. Today the secret would end.

Penny knew something was happening. She stood very still and let Felicity brush her.

"There, Penny, my beauty," Felicity said at last. "No one would recognize you. You're so clean and beautiful and so peaceful and calm."

Penny nudged her affectionately. Felicity rubbed

Penny's nose. "I love you, Penny," she said. "Are you ready?"

Penny stood next to the pasture fence and let Felicity climb on her back. Felicity wore her coral necklace for good luck. She wore her favorite gown, too, so that she and Penny would both look their best. "We're off, girl," Felicity said to Penny. "Now don't you worry. Everything will be fine."

The sun was rising, tinting the rooftops gold, as Felicity rode down the main street. The few people who were up stared and wondered. Was that the Merriman girl, riding astride a horse? And what a horse it was! A beauty! Where did such a horse come from?

coral necklace

Nan was carrying the breakfast bread from the kitchen to the house when Felicity rode into the yard. Nan's mouth fell open in astonishment. She called out, "Mother! Father! Come quick!"

"What's all the fuss and bother?" Mr. Merriman asked. He came outside wiping his face with a breakfast napkin. He stopped still when he saw Felicity riding Penny.

"Look!" cried William behind him. "Lissie's horse! Lissie's horse!"

"Felicity Merriman!" exclaimed Mother. "What are you doing? Where did you get that horse?"

"It's Penny," said Felicity. "It's the horse I told you about."

Ben came toward her. Penny stepped back nervously. "It's all right, Penny," said Felicity. "It's all right." She stroked the horse's neck, and Penny calmed down. Slowly, Ben reached up and touched Penny's neck.

"Is that the horse from Jiggy Nye's tannery?" asked Mr. Merriman. "What on earth are you doing with Jiggy Nye's horse? Does he know you have it? Why have you brought her here?"

"I wanted you to see her, Father," said Felicity quickly. "I wanted to show you how lovely and gentle she is. Penny was never vicious. It was only that Mr. Nye beat her and hurt her. She did not trust him—or anyone. She wouldn't let me ride her for the longest time."

"The longest time?" asked Mrs. Merriman. "Whatever do you mean? How long have you been . . . been going to her?"

"Near five weeks now," said Felicity. "Every morning."

Mrs. Merriman sank down on the step. "Five weeks? And we never knew!"

"But how did you tame her?" asked Mr. Merriman. "Who showed you what to do?"

"Penny herself. She showed me what to do," said Felicity. "All I had to do was to be patient and careful. I had to wait for her to trust me."

"She's a beautiful horse," said Mr. Merriman. "And she seems mild as a lamb. But she is not your horse to ride, even if you did tame her. You know it is wrong to borrow a horse without asking. You must take her back to the tannery now. You must apologize to Jiggy Nye for riding his horse. And you must never ride Penny again unless Jiggy Nye says that you may."

"But Father, you don't understand! I want to keep her!" cried Felicity. "I heard Mr. Nye say that anyone who could ride her could have her. I can ride her, so she's mine."

Mr. Merriman shook his head. "Lissie, Lissie," he said. "It is you who misunderstood. No one would give away a horse like this. She belongs to Jiggy Nye. You must return her."

"But he beats the horse and starves her," said Ben.

"That may be true, but it is still his horse," said Mr. Merriman firmly.

"Can't we buy her, Father?" begged Felicity. "Can't we keep her? Can't Penny stay?"

But Father had no time to answer. For at that moment, Jiggy Nye came reeling into the yard. Penny reared, and Felicity had to grab on to her mane to stay on her back. Nan shrieked and William wailed.

"I found ye!" yelled Jiggy. "Ye headstrong chit of a girl! You've stolen my horse! Get down off my horse!"

Felicity leaned down and threw her arms around Penny's neck. Penny was trembling. "You said anyone who could ride her could have her," Felicity said to Jiggy.

"I never did!" snarled Jiggy.

Nan cried out, "You did! You did! I heard you, you bad old man!"

Jiggy shouted, "I never meant no girl could steal that horse from me!"

"No one is trying to steal your horse," said Mr. Merriman. "My daughter misunderstood. She was wrong to take your horse, but it was a child's honest mistake. I make my apologies for her."

Mr. Nye shouted, "I never meant no girl could steal that horse from me!"

"Mistake!" said Jiggy. "Taking a horse is a crime!"

"The only crime here is the way you mistreat this horse," said Mr. Merriman. "You don't deserve to own Penny. I would buy her from you—"

"Hah!" shouted Jiggy. "Never! I will never sell this horse to you and your bold-faced daughter. The horse is mine, and it always will be mine. I can treat it any way I want to. Hear me? Now tell your brat to get off my horse before I rip her down myself!" he ordered.

"No!" cried Felicity. "Don't let him take Penny! Father, please don't!"

Mr. Merriman looked up at Felicity sadly. "Penny does not belong to you, Felicity. You must let Jiggy Nye take her."

Felicity held Penny tight. "Please, Father, please," she begged. "We can't let Penny go."

Mr. Merriman gently opened Felicity's arms and slid her off Penny's back.

Jiggy put a rope around Penny's neck and pulled it tight. He turned to Felicity and said, "Don't you come sneaking around! If I see you near this horse, I swear I'll kill it! I'll tan its hide before I let you touch it again."

Mr. Merriman put both his hands on Felicity's shoulders. "I'll not have you speak so roughly to my daughter, Nye. Be off with you!" he said.

Jiggy spat in the dust. Then he yanked on the rope and led Penny away.

Felicity felt dead inside. Penny was gone, and all her hopes were gone, too. "Penny!" she whispered. Then she turned and ran to the stable so that no one could hear her cry.

A while later, Father came into the stable to find her. Felicity was stroking Old Bess. She took comfort in Bess's warm, horsey smell.

Father put his arm around Felicity. "Have you cried all your tears, my child?" he asked.

Felicity nodded. They sat quietly for a while. Then Felicity said, "It was all a waste, wasn't it? It was all for nothing."

"Nothing?" said her father. "Didn't you tame that horse? Didn't I see you riding her, looking as fine as a queen?"

"But look how it ended," said Felicity. "Jiggy Nye has taken Penny back. I was wrong to ride off with her, and wrong to think that I could keep her. I was wrong to try to make her mine."

"No, Felicity, my dear," said Father. "It is never wrong to try to earn something you love. Indeed, 'tis only wrong not to try. You hoped for something and you put hard work behind your hope. I can only be proud of a daughter who can do that." He kissed Felicity's forehead. "You come back to the house when you're ready."

After Father left, Felicity pulled Ben's breeches out from under the bucket. She went to Ben's room and knocked. When he opened the door, Felicity held out his breeches. She said nothing.

Ben took the breeches. Suddenly he said, "Felicity, I have a little money. Maybe if we offered Mr. Nye money . . ."

"No, Ben," said Felicity. "You heard him say he will never sell Penny to us. He's too hateful."

"But Penny will never let Mr. Nye ride her," said Ben. "If he touches her, she'll go vicious again. Then he will beat her, and starve her, and soon I fear he'll—"

"He'll kill her, Ben," said Felicity.

"Aye," whispered Ben. "I fear he will."

"We've got to save her somehow," said Felicity. "We've got to. What can we do?"

"If only you could hide her somewhere," murmured Ben.

"Penny's not a horse that was meant to live hidden away," said Felicity. "She'd die of sadness if she were kept closed up in a stable or a pen."

"You are right," nodded Ben. "She'd be better off loose again, running free in the woods."

Felicity said softly, "Aye, she'd be better off running free." Then Felicity looked at Ben. "She'd be better off running free," she said louder.

Ben looked sad. "Felicity," he said slowly. "If you let her loose, you will never see her again."

Felicity nodded.

"And if you untie her and open the pasture gate and let her go, then that would be stealing," said Ben. "The punishment for horse theft is hanging."

Felicity nodded again. Without a word, she took the breeches out of Ben's hands and left.

❦

That night, Felicity didn't sleep at all. It was still dark, still the middle of the night when she crept out of bed, pulled on Ben's breeches, and ran along the familiar path to Penny's pasture.

The pasture gate was fastened shut with a heavy chain and lock, so Felicity climbed over the fence. She was surprised to see that Penny was not tied to the stake as she usually was. *Why didn't Mr. Nye tether her?* Felicity wondered. Felicity whistled softly, and Penny trotted over to her and nuzzled her hello. Felicity climbed onto Penny's back and whispered in her ear, "That's my girl, Penny. That's my fine one. Come on now, girl. Let's fly."

And just like all the mornings before, Penny trotted, then cantered, then galloped across the pasture. Faster and faster she flew. Felicity buried her face in Penny's mane and held on tight. Swiftly and smoothly, Penny sped across the pasture toward the tumble-down part of the fence. Felicity looked ahead and gasped in fear. The fence had been fixed! It loomed high and solid before them.

Penny can't jump that fence, Felicity thought. *It's too high.* But with one graceful leap, Penny jumped and sailed over the highest rail. And just as she did, just as she crossed the fence, Felicity let go of Penny's mane. She slipped off Penny's back and fell with a thud inside the pasture. Penny

Felicity looked ahead and gasped in fear. "Penny can't jump that fence," Felicity thought. "It's too high."

galloped on, carried by the force of her jump, running, running toward the woods. But just as she got to the edge of the trees, Penny stopped and looked back at the pasture where Felicity lay gasping for breath.

"Go on," whispered Felicity. "Go on, Penny. You are free."

Penny hesitated. She shook her mane and nickered. Then she disappeared into the woods.

"Good-bye, Penny. Good-bye, my girl," Felicity whispered. She sat on the cold ground and waited to be sure Penny was not going to come back. Felicity didn't care how late she was getting home. She didn't care if Mr. Nye found her there in the pasture. Penny was free now, and that was all that mattered.

At last Felicity stood, brushed the dirt off the breeches, and headed home. She was very weary.

Later that morning, Felicity went back to Ben's room above the stable. "Here are your breeches, Ben," she said.

Ben took the breeches. "Did you let her go?" he asked.

Felicity nodded. Her eyes filled with tears. "Penny is free," she said. "She freed herself."

"It's the best thing," said Ben.

"Aye," said Felicity. "But I hope she doesn't feel I've abandoned her. That would break my heart. She knows that I love her, doesn't she, Ben?"

"She knows," said Ben seriously. "She knows you love her so much you let her go free. You gave her what she needed most—her independence."

Felicity was quiet. Then she said, "Aye. That's it. Her independence."

❧

The next Sunday, as they were all setting out for church, Mrs. Merriman said, "Well, Ben! I see your friend returned those breeches at last! They're mended nicely, too."

"Yes, ma'am," said Ben.

"Mind you keep an eye on them, lad," said Mrs. Merriman.

"Yes, ma'am, I will," said Ben. "But if my friend should ever need them, I'd be honored to lend them again."

He and Felicity shared a secret smile.

A PEEK INTO THE PAST

AMERICA IN 1·7·7·4

The girl looking at you is Elizabeth Copley. She and her family were painted in 1777 by her father, John Singleton Copley, who is standing in the back.

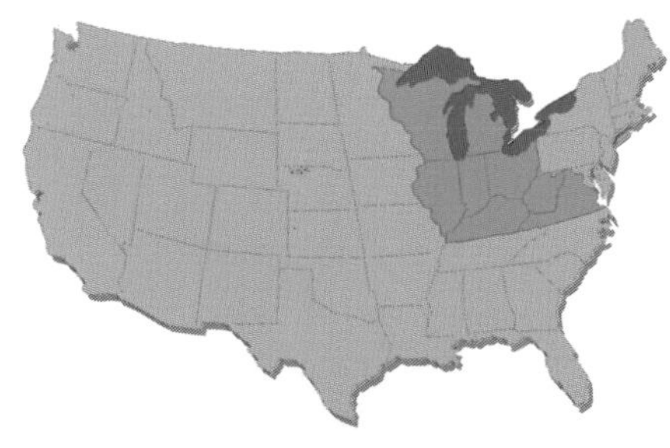

In 1774 the colony of Virginia claimed the dark green area on this map.

When Felicity was a young girl she lived in Virginia, one of the fifty states in the United States of America today. Back in 1774, Virginia was one of the thirteen colonies of England.

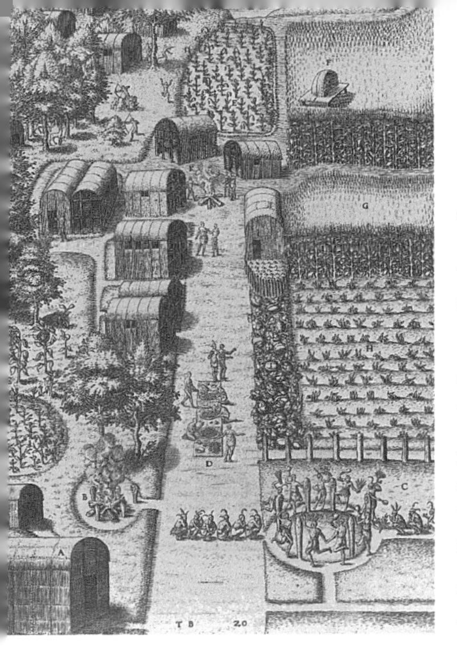

The first British colonists in Virginia saw Indian villages like this one. You can see dancing and feasting if you look closely.

A *colony* is a group of people who settle in a new land but follow a different country's laws. People came to the colonies so that they could have a better life, own land, or worship freely. But the English were not the first to settle in America, because Native American Indians had lived in America for at least 15 thousand years.

When Felicity was a young girl, most Virginia families lived on farms, but some lived in towns like Williamsburg. If you had walked down a street in Williamsburg, you would have seen a town buzzing with activity. Farmers came to town to sell their goods. Visitors came to see the latest English entertainments and fashions from Europe. Merchants came to do business. People who lived in the country came to shop at stores like Mr. Merriman's.

Farms in rural Virginia looked like this in Felicity's time.

This Colonial Williamsburg garden shows how wealthy colonists copied the patterns of gardens in England.

During Felicity's time, people liked things to be elegant, graceful, and orderly. Colonists built homes that were balanced, often with the same number of windows to the left and to the right of the front door. Gardens were also orderly, with flowers, fruit trees, and vegetables arranged in beautiful patterns.

Colonists' homes looked balanced from the front. Felicity's house would not have been as large as this one.

People's clothes showed how rich they were. Wealthy gentlemen wore velvet and silk suits with fancy trims. They wore pants called *breeches* that stopped at the knee, with silk stockings below. Gentlemen also wore wigs that were powdered, braided, and decorated with ribbons. Young boys, like Felicity's brother William, wore loose dresses until the age of four or five and then dressed like their fathers.

A man's wig.

In this painting by Stephen Slaughter, you can see how young girls of Felicity's age dressed.

Wealthy women wore long gowns made of many yards of fine fabric and lace. Under these gowns, they wore simple cotton shifts, and *stays* that fit tightly around their bodies to give a fashionable figure. Girls dressed like small copies of their mothers and wore stays from the time they were very young. People who were not so wealthy wore simpler clothes made from plainer material.

A humorous illustration showing stays being laced up. Sometimes women fainted from wearing such tight corsets.

A fashionable fan was part of a girl's outfit for any special occasion.

Dining was an art in colonial Virginia. Colonists took pride in setting an elegant table with a grand centerpiece. Virginia colonists loved to make visitors feel welcome with a beautifully set table. Dinner, served in the afternoon, consisted of at least two courses and sometimes lasted for many hours. There might be crabs and oysters from Chesapeake Bay, several kinds of meat, fruits, breads, vegetables of every kind, and, for dessert, fancy cakes, puddings, and tarts.

This elegant centerpiece is called an ***epergne*** *(ā–pairn). It held desserts like dried fruits and nuts, called "sweetmeats." Fancy plates had paintings of fruit, flowers, insects, and birds on them.*

The Shirley Plantation in Virginia is furnished in the style of the eighteenth century.

By COWPER & TELFAIRS,
A CARGO
of 170 prime
GUINEA SLAVES,
To be Sold at Private Sale,
THE PLANTATION

White landowners purchased Africans to work and live as their slaves in the colonies.

But not everyone in Williamsburg had fine food, elegant clothing, and beautiful homes. Half the people who lived in the town were African-American slaves, such as Marcus. They were forced to work long and hard for the person who owned them. They got little in return except basic food, clothing, and shelter.

An apprentice like Ben lived with a family for several years to work and learn a skill. However, an apprentice had the hope of a good life when the apprenticeship was over and he went out into the world to work on his own.

Today you can visit the town where Felicity grew up and see many of the buildings that were lived in long ago. Colonial Williamsburg is a "living history museum" open to visitors all year. You can taste colonial food and listen to music played on colonial instruments. You can see people dressed in colonial clothes and shop in colonial stores. You can pretend that you are Felicity living in the colony of Virginia more than two hundred years ago.

Today, Williamsburg welcomes thousands of visitors each year who come to see people working as they did in colonial times.